You are invited to:

Turtle and Snake's Spooky Halloween

by Kate Spohn

PUFFIN BOOKS

Happy Birthday, Terry!

PUFFIN BOOKS
Published by Penguin Group
Penguin Young Readers Group,
345 Hudson Street, New York, New York 10014, U.S.A.
Penguin Books Ltd, 80 Strand, London WC2R ORL, England
Penguin Books Australia Ltd, 250 Camberwell Road, Camberwell, Victoria 3124, Australia
Penguin Books Canada Ltd, 10 Alcorn Avenue, Toronto, Ontario, Canada M4V 3B2
Penguin Books (N.Z.) Ltd, 182-190 Wairau Road, Auckland 10, New Zealand

First published in the United States of America by Viking,
a division of Penguin Putnam Books for Young Readers, 2002
Published by Puffin Books, a division of Penguin Young Readers Group, 2003

3   5   7   9   10   8   6   4   2

THE LIBRARY OF CONGRESS HAS CATALOGED THE VIKING EDITION AS FOLLOWS:
Spohn, Kate.
Turtle and Snake's spooky Halloween / Kate Spohn.
p.   cm.
Summary: Turtle and Snake have plenty to do, including carving pumpkins
and brewing punch, before they host their Halloween party.
Includes recipe for Spooky Pond Punch.
ISBN 0-670-03560-2 (hardcover)
[1. Turtles—Fiction. 2. Snakes—Fiction. 3. Halloween—Fiction. 4. Parties—Fiction.]
I. Title: Turtle and Snake's spooky Halloween. II. Title.
PZ7.S7636 Yo 2002   [E]—dc21   2001006302 Rev.

Puffin Easy-to-Read ISBN 0-14-250078-X

Puffin® and Easy-to-Read® are registered trademarks of Penguin Group (USA) Inc.

Printed in China
Set in Bookman

Reading Level 2.0

Turtle and Snake are
planning a Halloween party.
They have a lot to do.

TO DO

1) invite friends

2) pumpkins

3) decorate

4) games

5) snacks

6) costumes

First they invite their friends.

"What's next?" asks Snake.

"Pumpkins," says Turtle.

So Turtle and Snake pick
pumpkins . . .

and make jack-o'-lanterns!

"What's next?" asks Turtle.
"We need to decorate,"
says Snake.

So Turtle and Snake decorate
Turtle's house.

"What's next?" asks Turtle.

TO DO

1) ~~invite friends~~

2) ~~pumpkins~~

3) ~~decorate~~

4) games

5) snacks

6) costumes ?

"Games!" says Snake.

16

So Turtle and Snake set up
the games.

"What's next?" asks Snake.
"Snacks!" says Turtle.

So Turtle and Snake buy
salty things

and sweet things.

Then they make
the snacks.

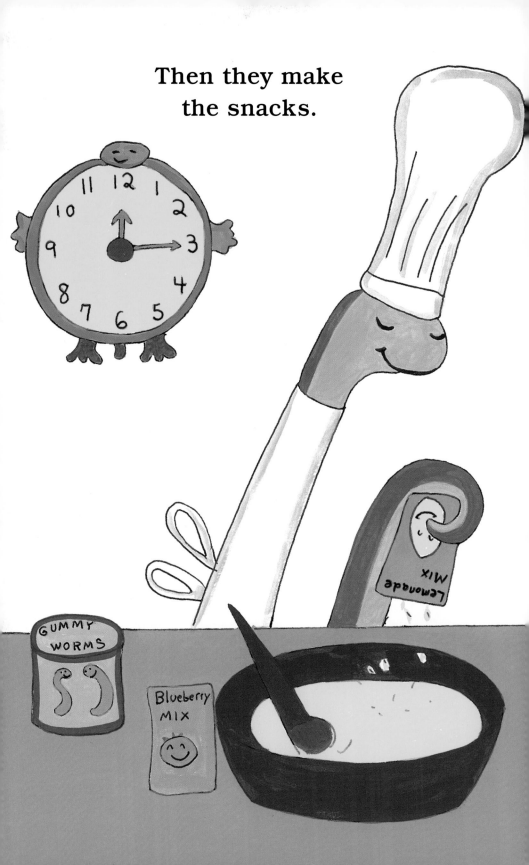

"What's next?" asks Snake.

"Costumes!" says Turtle.

So Turtle and Snake try on
costumes with wings

and costumes with capes,

but nothing seems right.

Then they see the perfect costumes!

It's Halloween night.
Everything is ready.
It's time for a party!

Who is on the left?
Who is on the right?

Welcome,

welcome all!

SNAKE'S SPOOKY BALL!

How to make

Turtle and Snake's
Spooky Pond Punch

You will need:

- 1 packet lemonade mix*
- 1 packet blueberry drink mix*
- Ice cubes
- Gummy worms

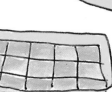

Make the lemonade.

Make the blueberry drink.

Mix them together in a punch bowl.

Add ice cubes.

Hang gummy worms over the
sides of the bowl.

*You could also use two packets
of lime-flavored drink mix.